A Screaming Kind of Day

A Screaming Kind of Day

BY **RACHNA GILMORE** • ILLUSTRATED BY **GORDON SAUVÉ**

Fitzhenry & Whiteside • *Toronto*

First published in the United States in 1999.

Fitzhenry & Whiteside acknowledges with thanks the support
of the Government of Canada through its Book Publishing Industry Development Program
in the publication of this title.

Printed in Hong Kong.
Cover and interior design by Wycliffe Smith Design

10 9 8 7 6 5 4 3

Canadian Cataloguing in Publication Data

Gilmore, Rachna, 1953-
A screaming kind of day

ISBN 1-55041-514-X

I. Sauve, Gordon. II. Title.

PS8563.I57S37 1999   jC813'.54   C99-930031-8
PZy.G54Sc 1999

For my mother, Shakuntala, with love
R.G.

—————————

Special thanks to Michelle and Kevin Hazzard whose spirit and energy inspired me,
and to their parents for their time and assistance.
Again thanks to my family, Barbara and Daniel for their love and support.
Gordon

It's a screaming kind of day.
I can tell the minute I open my eyes—
Leo's inches from my nose, making that
cross-eyed, twisty-mouth face.

He yanks my braid.

I don't bother to put in my hearing aids,
I leap out of bed.
I scream and chase him.

He turns around long enough for me to see his lips say,

    "Can't hear."

Then he keeps running. He's shouting something,
I can't tell what, but it's something piggy, I know it is,
wait 'til I get him.

Mom pulls us apart. Oh, oh, I forgot about her exams.

"Mom, it's all Leo's fault.
I didn't do anything, I…"

From Leo's mouth I catch something about the frog
in his sneaker, then he turns his head so I can't see,
and I hate it, he's lying, I bet he is.

"Time-out. Both of you," say Mom's lips.
Her face is hard, with those angry lines around her mouth.

"But Mom…" I start.
"Time-out," says Mom, looking me straight in the eye.

Her face says clearly, *don't mess with me*.

Leo's mouth starts to move and Mom turns to him.
From the look of him, he's getting it.
Serves him right— Mom turns around, sees my grin
and points to my room.

"Put in your hearing aids," her lips say.

It's a long morning. The clouds outside get heavier,
darker. It starts to come down misty.
Then it's raining thick and fast.
I want to go out.

I love the rain, the way the green sings with the rain.

I turn both hearing aids up all the way, to catch the sound.
There's a kind of whooshing.
Is that the rain?

I want to go out so bad.

I find Mom in the kitchen.

> "Mom, can I play in the rain?
> Please?"

Mom has this hurry, hurry look, she's flying around,
wiping the counter.

> "After lunch, Scully," she says.
> "If you're quiet this morning."

I wait. I wait hard.

14

At lunch time I chew with my lips closed, use my napkin
and speak softly. But Leo has to make faces at me and when
I pinch him under the chair he screams out loud, way loud,
even though it's a little pinch, and then he kicks me, so I have
to kick him back and—Mom pulls us apart and snaps,

"Back to your rooms."

I can tell she has a headache by the vein throbbing at the side
of her forehead.

Leo grins a *n'yah, n'yah* kind of grin.
He never plays in the rain,
he never even washes.

I go to my room and bang the door shut.
The rain skips and dances. It's leaping down, calling me.
I can hear it, I really can, *Scully, Scully, Scully,* a kind
of rushing, roaring.

I stick my head out the door and peer around.
Mom's in the living room, on the couch, surrounded by
her books.

I duck down low and sneak out the back door,
grabbing my rain coat off the hook.
I tie the hood down tight so my hearing aids won't get wet.

17

At last. I raise my hands high and lift my face to the rain.
It hops, laughing all over me.
I laugh and hop too.

Mom will be mad but I don't care,
the roaring wraps around me strong and wild.

I swing around and around.

Oh, oh. Someone at my window. Mom.
Her mouth is moving fast.
She looks straight at me and her hand waves *come here*.

I pretend I don't see and take off for the woods.

When I'm safe in the tent of green I stop.
It's all secret and shivery.
Rain skips and drips over me.
Maple leaves bounce,
the earth smells brown and sweet.

The green shouts out loud.

I whirl and whirl then flop to the ground,
let my arms listen to the rain shaking the earth.

Something towers over me. Mom.
She pulls me up.

   "Scully, you are in big trouble. I told you…," she says.

I won't listen.
I close my eyes and slump to the ground.
She pulls me up, I don't want to go, I won't.

I make the worst noise I can in her ear.

Mom makes me look at her face and says,

   "Don't do that again."

Even with the rain snapping around me,
I make out what she says.

23

In the kitchen, she lets go of my arm. Mom's hair
is stuck to her face— she's wet all the way through, right
to her temper.

Leo has this *you're in for it now* grin.

I put on my sweetest smile, the one with my head to the side,
like in my baby picture.

Mom says, "I love you too Scully, but you're grounded
for the rest of the day. Go to your room."

I yank off my hearing aids.

"Can't hear!"

Mom pulls me to my room. I scream.
Everything's sharp and gray, like bursting rocks, cutting glass.

I shout over and over, "I hate you."

My throat hurts. My wet clothes feel yucky.

I wipe my hearing aids and put them in.

At least they're still working.

I climb into bed and hug Blunder-Buss, my toy porcupine.
My eyes are tired from watching the rain cry.
I'm not sleepy, I'm not.

Mom's hands are soft on my hair,
but her face is still tired.
      "Did you have a good sleep, Scully?" she asks.

I nod.
I don't feel like screaming anymore.
I'm as still as deep blue water.

"Supper time," says Mom.

I can't believe I slept through the afternoon.
My stomach rumbles and roars.

It's my favorite spaghetti with Dad's bursting red tomato sauce.
Dad winks at me.

Leo doesn't have that nasty grin anymore.
He's too busy eating.

After dinner I sit by the open window.
No rain.
The sky is silky pink with licks of lavender.
The green smells full and glad.
I sigh and look at Mom.

"Can we go outside, Mom?
You know, wait for the stars?"

Mom looks at me for a long moment.
Then she smiles and that tight bit near her left eye
goes all soft.

She gets up and holds out her hand.
Maybe she does understand after all.
I put my hand into hers and squeeze.
I'm old enough I don't need to, but sometimes
Mom still does.

We go outside and sit on the picnic table.
I can feel the tired slipping, sliding out of Mom
'til she's easy as the wind.

The pink sky melts into red then blue,
darker, darker, calling night.

Leo comes out and stares at the sky too.
I'm all washed clean, not even a bit of mad.
I smile at him. He grins back and tweaks my braid.
It's a *you're okay, kid* kind of tweak.

I watch the sky go to sleep and the stars come out.
It's funny how they twinkle and flutter.
I turn my hearing aids all the way off.

If I'm very quiet, I might just hear the stars sing.

The author wishes to thank the following people:
Karleen Bradford, Jan Andrews, Caroline Parry and Alice Bartels
for their support and editorial feedback;
my agent Melanie Colbert for her enthusiasm and encouragement;
The Canadian Hard of Hearing Association, particularly Gladys Nielsen and Catherine Shearer,
as well as Vicki Robinson, of Voice, for their invaluable insights into Scully's world.